Tuck in the Pool

Story and Pictures by
Martha Weston

Clarion Books/*New York*

My thanks to Pamela Gompertz Schmitz, for her swim teacher expertise

Clarion Books
a Houghton Mifflin Company imprint
215 Park Avenue South, New York, NY 10003
Text and illustrations copyright © 1995 by Martha Weston

The illustrations for this book were executed in watercolor and pencil.
The text is set in 14/17-point New Aster.

Printed in the USA

Library of Congress Cataloging-in-Publication Data

Weston, Martha.
Tuck in the pool / story and pictures by Martha Weston.
p.   cm.
Summary: Tuck, a little pig taking swimming lessons, overcomes
his fear of the water with the help of his lucky rubber spider.
ISBN 0-395-65479-3
[1. Swimming—Fiction.   2. Fear—Fiction.   3. Pigs—Fiction.]   I. Title.
PZ7.W52645Tu   1995
[E]—dc20   94-7408
CIP
AC

WOZ 10 9 8 7 6 5 4 3 2 1

This book is for Charley

"Tuck! Time to go to swim class," said Tuck's mom.
"I'm busy," said Tuck.

"What are you busy doing?" asked his mom.
"I'm showing Snyder the dark."

Tuck crawled out clutching Snyder, his lucky rubber spider.
"I'm not going swimming," he told his mom.

"Why not?" she asked.

"They make you get your head wet so water gets in your ears
and it feels awful."

"You'll get used to that, Tuck," said Mom.
"Water gets in your eyes, too," said Tuck.
"And you'll get used to that, too," said Mom.

"Now hurry up. Your sister's all ready to go."
But Tuck just stood there looking at Snyder. Then he had an idea. He patted the spider and put it in his pocket.

"I love swim class," said Tuck's sister Bunny on the way to the
pool. "The kickboards are my favorite part. What do you like
best?"

"I like going home best," said Tuck.

Joyce, the instructor, blew her whistle. "Hop in, class," she shouted.

Tuck put his spider by the edge of the pool and patted it for luck.

Then he inched his way gingerly into the water.

"Let's see you all do ten bobs," said Joyce.
The class bobbed up and down. Tuck kept his ups high, but his downs only got his chin wet.

16

The students held on to the side of the pool and kicked their
feet. Then they hung on to kickboards and splashed across the
pool. Tuck patted Snyder two more times when no one was
looking.

"Your eyes are waterproof," said Joyce, as she gently pulled
Tuck along in the water. "Just blink them when they get wet."
But Tuck couldn't bring himself to try.

"Now, I want you each to hold on to the ladder, take a deep breath, and go underwater for as long as you can," said Joyce.

Tuck waited while the others took turns. He felt scared. Once his head had gone under accidentally and he'd swallowed water and it made him cough. What if that happened again?

"Tuck," said Joyce, "it's your turn."
"No, thank you," said Tuck.
"Come on, Tuck, you can do it."

Tuck held on tight to the ladder. Then, not caring if anyone saw, he turned to give Snyder a pat for luck.

"He's gone!" Tuck squealed.
"Who's gone?" asked Joyce.
"Snyder, my toy spider! He was right here!"

Suddenly Bunny called out, "Tuck! There it is!" And she pointed to the bottom of the pool.

"Snyder!" yelled Tuck, reaching into the water. It was too deep.

So he took a big breath, shut his eyes, and dove. The water closed over his head. But all he could think about was saving his spider.

Tuck groped around the bottom, but he couldn't find Snyder . . .

26

until he opened his eyes.

Hurray! Tuck popped up, clutching Snyder.
"Wow! You were under for six seconds!" said Joyce.
Tuck was sure it was more like six *hundred* seconds. He blinked the water out of his eyes and beamed with pride.
Joyce blew her whistle. Class was over.

"Guess what!" said Tuck when his mom got to the pool. "I went underwater! I got some water in my ears, but it came out."

"Oh, Tuck, I'm so proud of you!" said Mom, giving him a big hug.

The next day, when it was time for swim class, Tuck made sure Snyder was in his pocket.

"What if your spider falls in the water again?" asked Bunny.

"Then I'll just save him again," said Tuck.

Snyder didn't fall in during the lesson, and Tuck only needed to pat him once for luck.

But after the lesson, when Tuck and Bunny stayed for free swim, Snyder just couldn't seem to stay out of the water.